TORCHER
If found, please return to:
DR. ERNEST DRAKE
ST. LEONARD'S FOREST, HORSHAM

CONTENTS

An Introduction to Dragon Breeding...........1

Features of Different Breeds........................2

Starting Out...8

Feeding and First Aid................................12

Training...14

Educational Play..16

Communication..18

Dragon Milestones.....................................20

Leaving Home...22

Appendix I: Dragon Lullabies.....................24

Appendix II: A Dragon Record Book.........26

Afterword..30

Text and design copyright © 2005 by The Templar Company Plc.

Illustrations copyright © 2005 by Douglas Carrel

Designed by Jonathan Lambert and Nghiem Ta

Dragonology™ is a trademark of The Templar Company Plc.

All rights reserved.

First U.S. edition 2008

Library of Congress Cataloging-in-Publication Data is available.

Library of Congress Catalog Card Number pending

ISBN 978-0-7636-3652-4

2 4 6 8 10 9 7 5 3 1

Printed in China

www.ologyworld.com

PUBLISHER'S NOTE: This book purports to be the facsimile of an original that was among the effects of Dr. Ernest Drake. It is possible that he wrote it for two young apprentices who needed a little more information than was to be found in *Dragonology: The Complete Book of Dragons*, said to have been originally published in 1895 and republished by Candlewick Press in 2003.

CANDLEWICK PRESS
CAMBRIDGE, MASSACHUSETTS

visit us at www.candlewick.com

DR. ERNEST DRAKE'S

Dragonology™

BRINGING UP
BABY DRAGONS

A GUIDE FOR BEGINNERS

Dragonology™

EDITED BY

DUGALD A. STEER, B.A. (BRIST), S.A.S.D.

ILLUSTRATED

CANDLEWICK PRESS
PUBLISHERS OF RARE & UNUSUAL BOOKS

*Few hobbies are quite so absorbing as
hatching and raising baby dragons.*

An Introduction to Dragon Breeding

———— ❦ ————

There has been much talk of dragons recently and a great deal of rummaging about in hedgerows, going on expeditions to remote mountain caves, exploring lost jungle cities, and setting off on trips to the icy wastes around the poles in search of them. At the Secret and Ancient Society of Dragonologists, this has been a cause of some anxiety, in case a dragon should fall into the hands of someone who lacks the knowledge and experience to care for it properly. Few hobbies are quite so absorbing as hatching and raising baby dragons, but there are not many pursuits that require such total care and dedication. It was with this in mind that I penned this guide to dragon rearing. *Bringing Up Baby Dragons* will teach you all you need to know about dragon care, from choosing the right breed and preparing a lair to releasing your companion back into the wild. Whether you choose to adopt an orphan dragon chick or hatch one from an egg, this trusty guide is one that you'll be sure to refer to again and again.

Ernest Drake

FEATURES OF
DIFFERENT BREEDS

When selecting the best breed of dragon to raise, one must consider various factors: if one lives in an apartment or a house, if one has a yard, if one lives in town or in the country, how much exercise one can give the dragon, if there are children at home, and if one can keep it securely.

EUROPEAN *Draco occidentalis magnus*
THE most well-known breed, the European dragon needs a large, secure home with a considerable acreage of grounds, or at least a handy forest, if buildings are not to be torched willy-nilly and friends and neighbours not frightened, or worse.

*TORCHER
THE MIGHTY*

The charcoal brazier used to keep a European dragon's egg hot must be kept in a well-ventilated location.

KNUCKER *Draco troglodytes*

ONE of the few choices for those who live in an apartment, the knucker is one of the smaller dragons. However, its tendency to eat anything when hungry means that it should not be kept where there are very young babies.

WEASEL

A knucker's egg may be kept warm on top of an ordinary stove.

FROST *Draco occidentalis maritimus*

RAISING a frost dragon from the egg is only an option for those who live within the Arctic Circle. Frost chicks can tolerate warm temperatures, but staying above freezing for too long tends to make them sluggish, so the use of heating at home is not recommended.

SPITZ

A frost dragon's egg must be kept as cold as possible. The arrangement of a fan and a block of ice can help.

3

ASIAN *LUNG*
Draco orientalis

LUNG WEI

THE proximity of running water is essential to the raising of *lung* chicks. Only attempt to raise them if you live near a stream, waterfall, or suitable river.

Underwater breathing apparatus is required for tending lung *eggs.*

WYVERN *Draco africanus*

TO raise a wyvern chick, just remember this simple rule: Give it *plenty* of exercise. Take it on many walks and bring it to the park frequently. A wyvern chick rarely tires.

SALAZAR

A sturdy wheelbarrow will assist considerably in moving wyvern eggs, should the need ever arise. Be very careful not to drop the eggs onto your toes.

4

GUSANO

MEXICAN AMPHITHERE

Draco americanus mex

ONE of the more exotic breeds, this chick will feel at home in a pyramid-shaped nest built of brick or stone. It loves humid conditions.

A Mexican amphithere's egg has a rubbery shell and can be bounced without harming the embryo inside.

HOPPY

A high degree of variation in patterning on marsupial eggs helps a mother dragon to identify her clutch.

MARSUPIAL *Draco marsupialis*

EASY to both hatch and raise, the marsupial dragon had no known natural enemies until the coming of man to Australia. Should a chick ever show signs of distress, the best remedy is to mimic its natural Blue Mountains environment by splashing a lot of eucalyptus oil about. 5

RARE AND EXOTIC BREEDS

In addition to the common varieties of dragons described on the previous pages, some breeders prefer to specialise in the raising of rare dragons to release back into the wild. Others prefer to test their dragon-rearing skills by raising hazardous exotica such as the cockatrice.

COCKATRICE *Gallicus halitosis*

INCREDIBLY dangerous because of the power of its fatal breath, the cockatrice presents an unusual challenge to the home breeder. A mask made of tightly woven silk dipped in a powerful stink-retardant is the very least requirement when dealing with this creature.

A large tame toad will be required in order to help your baby cockatrice hatch out properly.

No one is sure why a toad is needed to hatch a cockatrice egg, but its warty skin may play a part.

BOG–CROW

AMERICAN AMPHITHERE

Draco americanus tex

THE rare American amphithere is prized by breeders for its fur, which comes in a wide variety of colours. It is the dream of some breeders to hatch a chick with a "Stars and Stripes" pattern.

The shell of Draco americanus tex *gives off a phosphorescent glow that helps a parent to locate it.*

LEATHERJAW

These extremely resilient eggs can be dropped from a tremendous height with no ill effects of any kind.

PETITES-DENTS

GARGOUILLE *Draco occidentalis minimus*

HANDY for those who live in one of the new high-rise apartment buildings that seem to be springing up, the gargouille will sit happily on a windowsill or balcony for days without moving a muscle, giving every appearance of being part of the building.

STARTING OUT

There are two main ways of rearing dragons: obtaining an orphan chick or hatching an orphan egg. Never attempt to hatch an egg or rear a chick that is not an orphan—the mother dragon will find you sooner or later, and unpleasantness may very easily result.

WHERE TO OBTAIN AN EGG OR CHICK

The Wild: Not recommended unless you can be quite sure the egg or chick is a genuine orphan who needs your help.

A Shady Dealer: Not recommended unless you are an expert at telling a good egg from a bad one. Some dealers sell chicks, then steal them back again.

The Secret and Ancient Society of Dragonologists: The best way to guarantee quality, but the waiting list is extremely long.

A Registered Dragon Breeder: Sadly, the scarcity of dragons has driven many breeders out of business.

Beware of offers from shady dealers on Shadwell Dock.

KNOWING A GOOD EGG

To be sure you haven't been given a false dragon's egg, perform these tests: Does it sink in boiling water? (It should.) Does it dissolve in acid? (It shouldn't.) Can you unwrap it? (If you can, it's an Easter egg.)

RAISING FROM THE EGG VERSUS ORPHAN ADOPTION

In general, it is better to raise a chick from the egg. It is easier to form a firm bond with a just-hatched chick than with one that is sure to be missing its mother.

PREPARING YOUR HOME FOR THE NEW ARRIVAL

Before introducing a dragon chick into your home, you must make sure that anything really valuable is out of harm's way. Chicks chew, claw, and scratch; are quite likely to steal shiny objects to hide; and may attempt to set fire to flammable objects. Make sure you have adequate stocks of food. It is also important to set up a "home base" for the new arrival, so that you can get to know each other safely.

If it is too bothersome to set up a lair indoors . . .   *make sure that your yard is fenced in.*

HATCHING FROM AN EGG

Having obtained your egg, take it home as quickly as possible in order to keep it warm. Then place it on a nest of live coals, which must be kept burning during the incubation period of 36 months. In the early months, it is important to turn the egg each day, so that the yolk inside does not stick to the inner shell.

1. Be Prepared.
European dragon eggs take 1,095 days to incubate. If you know when yours was laid, you can predict when it will hatch.

2. Listen for Knocking.
As soon as the dragon chick is ready to hatch, it will begin tapping on the shell with its egg horn.

3. Smash Severely.
Help Baby hatch by smashing the shell with a sledgehammer. Do not repeat once Baby is hatched.

4. Fetch Hatching Tools.
Useful hatching tools include a sledgehammer to help crack the eggshell, hot water and towels to clean the newborn chick, and tongs to grasp it.

5. Bond with Baby.
Wash the baby with the hot water, wrap it in a towel, and bond with it. "Coochie-coochie-coo!"

DRAGON CHICK DOS AND DON'TS

These dos and don't apply to newly hatched chicks, who are, as you will find, rapid developers. Remember: If you can keep your head while everything burns around you, you'll be a dragonologist, my son.

DO:

* Refer to yourself as "Mommy" or "Daddy."
* Place some shiny objects in the chick's new "lair."
* Spend time with your new chick each day.
* House-train your new chick as quickly as possible.
* Keep your chick fed.

DON'T:

* Refer to your sister as "Breakfast" or "Dinner."
* Leave iron and flint objects lying around.
* Leave your chick alone for weeks on end.
* Ignore "bad" behaviour — deal with it as it happens.
* Run out of food.

FEEDING AND FIRST AID

Most experienced dragonologists know that a 40- to 50-acre farm with a head of 300 cows should be just about enough for one chick. However, it is useful to vary the dragon's diet from time to time, to make sure that it gets all the essential minerals and nutrients that it needs to grow.

RECIPES FOR SUCCESS

These recipes show how a dragon's favourite snacks can easily be incorporated into its meals. Please avoid including animals such as polar bears and elephants, which require conservation themselves.

FROST DRAGON RECIPE
"POLAR BEAR" PIE

Ingredients:
150 oily fish such as mackerel
10 gallons white sauce
Parsley to garnish
[Never use real *polar bears.]*

Place all the fish in a receptacle such as a 25-gallon cauldron, add white sauce and parsley, and freeze solid.

MARSUPIAL RECIPE
KANGAROO COBBLER

Ingredients:
15 plump kangaroos
24 pairs old leather shoes
2 sacks whole-grain flour
6 pounds butter

Saute the shoes until tender. Rub the butter into the flour. Add the minced kangaroos to the shoes, top with flour, and bake.

THE IMPORTANCE OF PHYSICAL EXERCISE

Some first-timers are shocked to find that dragon chicks are quite energetic and need plenty of physical exercise. Unless it is able to let off steam (and smoke, and sometimes bursts of flame, too), the chick's natural exuberance may turn destructive. Should this happen, saying "No!" in a firm voice is unlikely to make much of a difference.

Make sure the chick knows what it is supposed to fetch.

BASIC FIRST AID

As soon as you note the tell-tale sad looks and general "droopiness" of an unwell dragon, make sure that you wrap it up and provide it with lots of loving care and attention. A dragonological veterinarian may be called if things worsen rapidly.

TRAINING

Dragons are not particularly easy to train, nor is it recommended to train them excessively, given that they must be released back into the wild as soon as they are old enough. However, there are a few things that can be done to make living with your new chick a great deal easier—particularly as regards house-training.

Luckily, dragons become house-trained after two or three years.

DR. DRAKE'S DRAGON-TRAINING TIPS

DRAGON MESS

Adult dragons do not make a mess in their own lairs, but chicks need to develop control. Until they do, cover the whole floor with a good 2 feet of paper to soak up the mess.

FIRE-BREATHING

If you go out and leave your chick at home, it will not burn down your house to punish you but rather because it is anxious. Make sure it has lots of toys to incinerate instead.

REWARDS

While there is little point to punishments—they will just make the dragon sulky and, in more extreme cases, vengeful—there is plenty of reason to provide a good dragon who is exhibiting desired behaviours with tasty rewards.

OTHER BEHAVIOURS

As your dragon matures, it will take a different sort of interest in the world around it. For example, at first, a chick may find books interesting, but only from the perspective of how brightly they burn. Do not take it to a library at this stage. After the chick has learned to read, it will no doubt adore books, but by then you are unlikely to be able to find a librarian who will let it in.

LEAPING UP

While no one minds a baby dragon leaping up at him or her, a fully grown adult is another matter. Make sure you push the chick away from you firmly and say "No."

ROARING

When your dragon roars, praise it for raising the alarm and offer it a treat. Gradually make sure that it stops roaring for at least a minute before it gets the treat.

If you have a female chick, you may find that she steals ordinary hens' eggs from your kitchen so that she can pretend they are her own. She will not damage them, but when you retrieve them, you will find that they are all quite perfectly cooked.

15

EDUCATIONAL PLAY

Like many young animals, dragon chicks learn a number of their adult behaviours through play of various sorts. Mock battles are common, but as dragons have a flameproof skin and you most likely do not, it is wise to initiate games that are as safe as possible.

GAME ONE—HIDE AND EAT
This game teaches hunting. Hide food around the yard for the chick to find. Note that one should not play this game until the chick knows the difference between "food" (for example, a bone) and "not food" (for example, your next-door neighbours).

Make sure that all the food is well hidden.

GAME TWO—LEAPDRAGON
Dragon siblings often play a game called leapdragon. As they use their wings to leap over each other, their flight muscles are gently stretched and exercised. It is not a good idea to play this game with older chicks, as they can be too heavy, but it can prove entertaining with younger ones.

A well-fed dragon chick can make the ideal playmate for energetic children.

COMMUNICATION

AN INTRODUCTION TO DRAGON SIGNING

Research suggests that dragon chicks can recognise and use simple signs much sooner than they can talk. Dragon signing lets you communicate with a chick long before its vocal cords have developed.

Dear little Torcher makes his very first "Treasure" sign.

BASIC TECHNIQUE

There are no hard-and-fast rules about dragon signing, although the signs I suggest here have proved useful. They have been developed so that both dragons and humans find them reasonably easy to make. Simply make sure that the dragon sees you making the appropriate sign at any given time, and it will soon begin to copy you.

Food

Not food

Treasure

Attack

Lair

Good dragon

When it is time to move on from dragon signing and learn first words, you may create your own teaching materials or else choose those available in the BabyDrake collection.

MY FIRST DRAGON ABC from *BabyDrake*

A is for *Amulet.*

C is for *Claw.*

D is for *Diamond.*

B is for *Bone.*

E is for *Egg.*

DRAGON MILESTONES

After the "honeymoon period" of the first year, when a properly supervised dragon chick makes a delightful companion, the dragon's wild nature is more and more in evidence until the end of the fifth year, when, fully grown, it must finally be released back into the wild.

THE TERRIBLE TWOS

THE "Terrible Twos" are so named because the dragon will have grown fairly large but will not yet have become house-trained. Keep a shovel by the door until the chick learns that certain activities must be done outside.

THE TRAUMATIC THREES

DURING this stage—which is not at all traumatic for the dragon chick—the dragon first begins to show signs of hoarding behaviour. Shiny objects will be collected from relatives, visitors, and neighbours and will be defended in an energetic way. Luckily, a three-year-old dragon will not yet be able to produce fire effectively. However, it is still probably safer to wait for a moment when the dragon is distracted—or fast asleep—before attempting to reclaim any stolen goods.

THE FRUSTRATING FOURS

THE "Frustrating Fours" actually are frustrating for the dragon itself. During this period, it undergoes a growth spurt, which tends to make it lose its natural gracefulness. Additionally, it is during the fourth year that most dragons attempt to fly—often with hilarious results. However, it is usually better not to laugh too loudly.

If at first you don't succeed, fly, fly, and fly again. . . .

THE FRIGHTFUL FIVES

IT is a brave dragonologist who is able to endure a full-blown episode of the "Frightful Fives," when a dragon, still an inexpert flyer, becomes restless. It is at this time that fire is finally produced with ease—a clear sign that the dragon is nearing maturity and must soon leave the "nest."

LEAVING HOME

RELEASING A DRAGON INTO THE WILD

At last the time comes that all dragonologists dread—when the chick we have cared for so much has grown too large and savage to be looked after at home and must be released into the wild. Do not forget that our main aim is the protection and conservation of *wild* dragons.

NEW HOME CHECKLIST

* Far from human beings
* Plentiful food supply
* No other dragons nearby
* Large enough area
* Possible lair sites nearby
* Not too hard to visit
* The right habitat for the dragon you are releasing

It is importants to be firm when releasing a dragon into the wild. At first it may not understand why it has to go.

After only a few hours, you will find that the dragon is completely at home in its new environment.

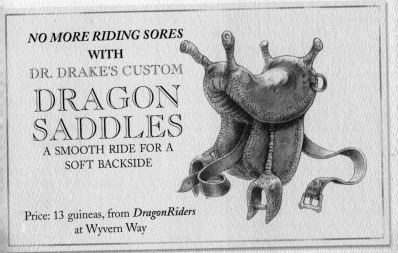

APPENDIX I

DRAGON LULLABIES

Sometimes dragon chicks find it difficult to settle in to a new home. On such occasions, traditional lullabies may prove useful. Remember that the chick may well not understand the words you use so much as the tone of your voice, which must be as loud and deep as possible.

HUSH, LITTLE WYVERN

Hush, Little Wyvern;
don't say a word,
Mama's gonna find you
an elephant herd.
If those elephants
are eaten by spring,
Mama's gonna find you
a diamond ring.

ROUND AND ROUND THE CASTLE

Round and round the castle,
like an amphithere,
a-one puff, a-two puff,
we'll burn it down from here.

Round and round the castle,
like an angry wyrm,
we'll give a roar,
and then some more,
and watch the people squirm!

ROCK-A-BYE, DRAGON

Rock-a-bye, Dragon
on the hilltop.
A knight will ride by,
but then he will stop.

When that knight stops,
the dragon will roar,
and the knight will not ever
go there anymore.

ITSY-BITSY DRAGON

Itsy-bitsy dragon
climbed down the magma spout.
Up came an eruption
and blew the dragon out.
Down came the lava,
just like a shower of rain.
Then Itsy-bitsy dragon
climbed down the spout again.

THREE BLIND KNIGHTS

Three blind knights.
Three blind knights.
See how they run!
See how they run!
They all ran after the
knucker chick,
who gave each one a
venomous lick.
Did you ever hear
of a sillier trick
than three blind knights?

TWINKLE, TWINKLE

Twinkle, twinkle, little star;
how I wonder what you are.
Up above the world so high,
like a diamond in the sky.
Could I fetch you if I soared?
And bring you back to swell
my hoard?

WEE WILLIE WYVERN

Wee Willie Wyvern
flies through the town.
Huffing and puffing,
he's going to burn it down.
Scratching at the window,
clawing at the lock:
"Are the children in their beds?
They're going to get a shock!"

APPENDIX II
A DRAGON RECORD BOOK

Every dragonologist loves to record those extra-special moments in their chick's life for posterity. Below you can see a sample of such a record—on the next page there is a blank version that you may copy to use yourself.

NAME:	Torcher
DRAGON TYPE:	European
AGE:	2 years
WEIGHT AT BIRTH:	15 pounds
LENGTH AT BIRTH:	1 foot 8 inches

FAVOURITE FOOD:	The whole hog
FAVOURITE TOY:	My flameproof cloak
FIRST STEPS:	2 hours old
FIRST SIGNS OF HOARDING BEHAVIOUR:	At 2 hours 2 minutes old, he stole my pocket watch. Is this a record?
FIRST WORDS:	"Eat," "Boy," "Treasure"
FIRST FLAME:	2 hours 3 minutes old

OTHER NOTES: Torcher is a very inquisitive little fellow, but he rather lost his spark the day he felt poorly. Luckily, he was soon up and about again after a dose of my specially formulated linctus. It is amazing how he seems to know when it is Sunday lunchtime. You've got to watch him like a hawk in the kitchen!

MY DRAGON RECORD BOOK

Begin your records by making a sketch of your very own dragon in the box below.

NAME:

DRAGON TYPE:

AGE:

WEIGHT AT BIRTH:

LENGTH AT BIRTH:

FAVOURITE FOOD:

FAVOURITE TOY:

FIRST STEPS:

FIRST SIGNS OF
HOARDING BEHAVIOUR:

FIRST WORDS:

FIRST FLAME:

OTHER NOTES:

AFTERWORD

Remember that the study of dragons—with a view to their conservation and protection—can be the start of a lifetime of scientific adventure. If you need more information, I suggest you read my books *Dragonology,* *The Dragonology Handbook,* and *A Field Guide to Dragons,* which are all available to members of the Secret and Ancient Society of Dragonologists.

Ernest Drake